Unquenchable Desires

FanatiXx Publication

ISO 9001:2015 Certified

FanatiXx Publication

AM/56, Basanti Colony, Rourkela 769012, Odisha

ISO 9001:2015 CERTIFIED

Website: *www.fanatixx.in*

"Unquenchable Desires"

ISBN: 978-93-90117-10-9

English Poems 1st Edition

Book Formatting: Saizal Gupta

Cover Design: Sagar Samal

Disclaimer

This is a work of fiction. Names, characters, places, and incidents are either the product of author's imagination or have been used illustratively and any resemblance to any person, living or dead, events or locales is entirely coincidental.

Udaigiri Amravathi asserts all rights to be identified as the author of this work.

Acknowledgement

Thank you to everyone I have ever met, my experiences with you all, good and bad have dug me to depths in knowing and shaping myself who I am for better or worse. Sincere thanks to my parents, special thanks to Sandeep Kurukunda and the team FanatiXx publication who have not only put up with all my craziness but also encouraged it. FanatiXx took a step forward in encouraging and displacing my talent to the outer world with great ease and enthusiasm. You guys helped me grow better in selecting the relevant stuff which could enhance not only my work but standards too and an immense thanks to all my readers out there for sparing your precious times to peep in and read my content which I poured out of my soul.

Contents

Accolades to thy Almighty 1

One Pulse of Passion 3

Tale of thought residing in my heart............. 5

Longing for love license 7

Unbridled needs.. 9

Zeal ought to Reveal..................................... 11

Trials that Revile 13

Elegant loot 15

Petrified Emotions 17

Mystic Magnetism.. 19

Internal echoes... 21

Malaise Grace 23

My mysterious malefactor 25

Entangled in you 27

Adroit delicacy 29

Love that's Extraordinaire 31

Intuitive insights 33

Sweet Surrender 35

Stolen Innocence.. 37

Unfathomable emotions............................... 39

Passion paradise... 41

Only goal is his soul.................................... 43

Shadows of my past..................................... 45

Sole Soul of my Life 47

Heart's flight.. 49

Accolades to thy Almighty

Praise to thy begetter for his serene efforts,

Brought thee into cosmos through all comforts.

Had he ain't speculate of what he made,

Of all the charms and charisma, he laid.

Thee that amaze with your every gaze,

I plat your praise in every phrase.

"You set me ablaze……..

With your every gaze…….."

One Pulse of Passion

You set my heart on fire,

Fill my veins all with desire.

Deliberate that you make me wait,

Let's celebrate for the night we mate.

My eyes flicker on your sight,

That's lethal than a liquors plight.

Mutate my thoughts with all your grace,

Amputate this distance not leaving even a trace.

Delight is your every move O' Dear,

That holds my breath hard to bear.

"Desire that's always on fire......

Forces that let me admire...."

Tale of thought residing in my heart

With all your sheen,

You catch up my keen.

Letting me admire your aesthetic senses,

Held all with charming suspense's.

Your figure makes my oxytocin sprint,

With the plunge of vasopressin tint.

Let I make the same sins again,

Your beauty stings me making me abstain.

Nudge me down trimming up this space,

Let I be drown swimming up this grace.

"The love ought to be created by us……
An attire to be experienced……….."

Longing for love license

Rid me from this plague of silence,

Bid me giving your love license.

Lost to extreme that I in your vortex,

Most of me left all in perplex.

Sever these chains of solitary dearth,

Cheer my soul stuffing your love girth.

Imprint this being with all your memories, O'Love,

Let's blueprint our being in a dwelling abode.

"Want you more than.......
I want to breathe......."

Unbridled needs

Aimed to wound me is his athletic gaze,

Leaving me bound to dream our days.

His face has shackled my patient brain,

Sight that simmered my blood like cocaine.

Had I should be jittered to gain his elusive arms,

I'm sure I would be glittered in my illusive charms.

"Dig me till the depths.........
Crave me till the sweats......."

Zeal ought to Reveal

Unfailingly in my dreams,

I want to see you in my arms.

It's hard but if I could only reveal,

Let I love you with all my zeal.

Often that tells my inner voices,

You are the one my heart rejoices.

Lucid are your eyes hiding all the love within,

Stupid I ain't but I'll love you even if it's a sin.

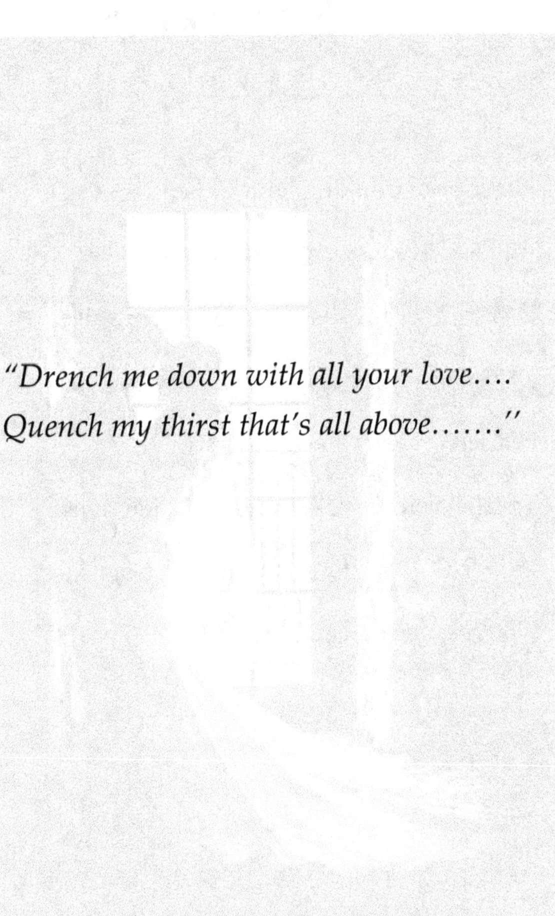

"Drench me down with all your love….
Quench my thirst that's all above……."

Trials that Revile

I have been thinking for a while,

All I would sense is you meanwhile.

Everything that fills me is you worthwhile,

Driven in my thoughts is your smile.

Hidden grace in you is your style,

To fetch your love, I can walk million mile.

Your 'NO' to my love can turn me fragile,

Life without you could be an exile.

*"Compiled erratic emotions on you make
me imbecile…....
Smile of yours made all the admirers
immobile…...."*

Elegant loot

I feel like I am always dreaming,

Inside me my inner voices screaming.

Had I got to owe him through occult practices?

Thoughts nod that's Okay to do for such artpieces.

Or do I need to abduct him when he's asleep?

More I feed myself with disrupting ideas that

creep.

Outlet of all the coziness to win him endeavor,

Let this craziness on him in me last forever.

"My body quivers when his motions heard.......
After all he is an outcome of all the emotions sculptured......."

Petrified Emotions

Your sight hit my heart with a speed of locust swarm,

You are the one, Lord created with all the mystic charm.

Doer might guilt in thought for making you so hot and warm,

Your shoe steps on the stairs seem to me as fire alarms.

Can't you show mercy on me by aiding no harm?

You lynched me to the deathblow with your gracious form.

"He inked me with his edified titillates…...
Luridly provoking me for a blind
date……"

Mystic Magnetism

A vision that throbs inside me for several years,

This prison of restraint seems no more appears.

Cherished from inside my soul onto him adheres,

A whole series of unknown tunes rhythm discovers.

Sort of illusion wafts in eyes like a crystal clear prism,

Ultimately unhitched is my soul from his magnetism.

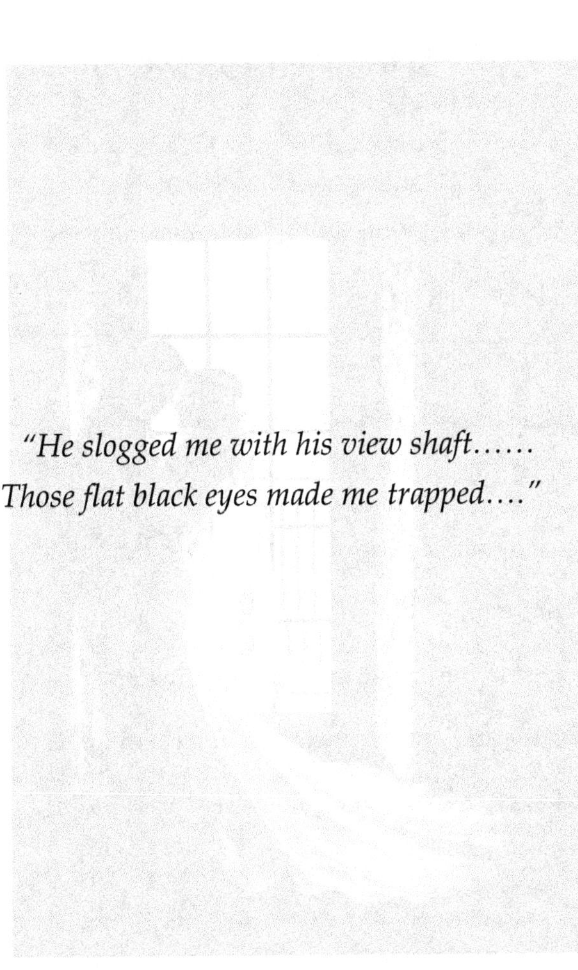

"He slogged me with his view shaft……
Those flat black eyes made me trapped…."

Internal echoes

Setting fire on nerves that his aroma unknown,

Unwinking my eyes, I saw the king without crown.

In between the drizzle of the dusky sun,

Magic spells rendering on me of meaning

unknown.

I have noticed the man beset in the butterflies

flattering,

Lost in the crowd, my heart is withering.

His cold sight touched my soul mellowing,

I pray, this moment should ever last unfading.

"He must have built in his own
strategy……..
Motive to steal me through his soul's
mastery……."

Malaise Grace

You stole my heart with great ace,

Do steal my soul unleaving even a trace.

Give me all your hidden grace,

Drew I not from your love lace.

Hit onto me is your deity face,

Bit unleft in me even a mighty space.

*"Your glamour is a mirror maze……
Symmetry born with floral glaze……"*

My mysterious malefactor

Marvelous is your physique with sturdy built,

Venomous are your eyes that spear me like a hilt.

Clueless is your crime that's hard to implore,

Mysterious is your form that's hard to ignore.

Caught is my breath that's about to cease,

Thought that raise to accomplish a fease.

Futile that it seems until it's done,

Utile is this effort unless you're twenty-one.

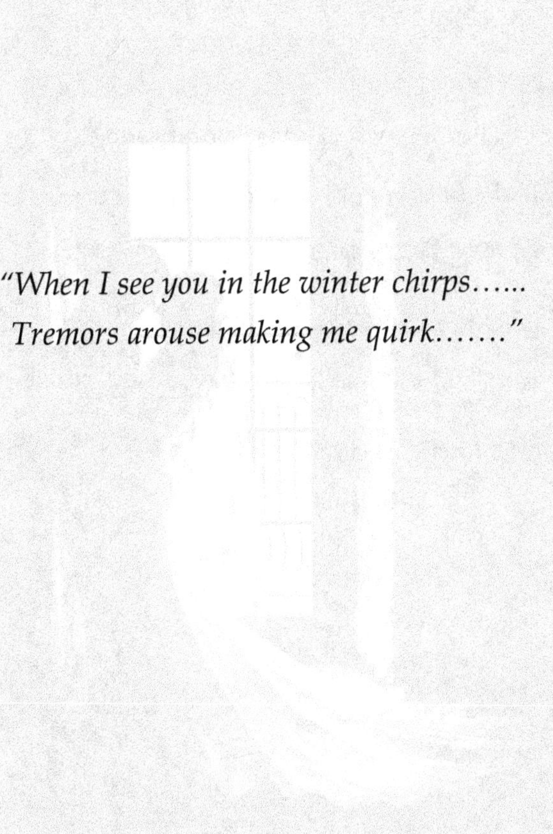

"When I see you in the winter chirps…....
Tremors arouse making me quirk……."

Entangled in you

Tangled in my soul is your beauty adorn,

Baffled I ain't but I myself sworn.

Not to lose this eternal ardor left,

Ought to acquire by a skillful theft.

Wish you owe me a clement full approach,

Miss I not even a remnant abroach.

"Thoughts tamed to adore you…
Unframed with the only aim and its
'You'…."

Adroit delicacy

Discreet was I for expressing my love for you,

Concrete I turned with the flash of light shot from

you.

Mesmerized from every bottom of your pretty

plight,

Anesthetized me your gentle eyes.

Extemporized was my outcome on your jiffy sight,

Unable to trace where the error lies.

"Visualized that I our date......
Organized at a sky height........."

Love that's Extraordinaire

Often that reverberates is your name in my ear,

Happen to accelerate leaving hard to bear.

Is it tough to negate this distance, O'Dear,

Let's instigate our relation making it rare.

Bet I declare that I'll love you extraordinaire,

Don't you deprecate leaving me in despair.

"Let I dare to make you my pair......
The love we share, it's going to be rare...."

Intuitive insights

Scintillating sky is your each eye,

Forging me desperate to die.

Preserved emotions that I want you to know,

Reserved is you in my heart that I'll never let go.

Before it's too late, heal me down,

Why don't you just steal me and make your own.

Perceive all my intuitive insights,

Believe me I will love you outright.

"Heal me down……….
Before I frown……....."

Sweet Surrender

Embrace my heart with kind perusal,

Unlace this being from thought eschewal.

Elixir is your approval in my life, O'Dear,

Revere that I linger to thrive I swear.

Turf veiled in mist shall make our tryst,

Swerve to sway that I holding your wrist.

"I owe to see you every morning
mist………
That's the only desire so far exist……….."

Stolen Innocence

You stole my innocence and made me bold,

Do steal my essence unnerved in cold.

Falling for your prey my emotions swoon,

Fawning to lay on the oceans of lagoon.

I yearn for your every somnolent curve,

Burn my intentions with your dominant verve.

Enticing within is a smattering romance,

Clinging for indulgence in sensual pleasures.

"I strive to hold..........
Onto your beautiful soul........."

Unfathomable emotions

Injurious is your augmentative adorn countenance,

Delirious I turn admiring your conscient appearance.

Lecherous thoughts haunt me at your every glance,

Lascivious aims shot in heart aiding no chance.

Erroneous it's ain't to even die to get you,

Obvious I am woven to rely onto you.

Unfathomable emotions arouse on your gaze of grey eyes,

Infallible trails I make to create a fervid paradise.

"Compelled to get hypnotized in your eyes…...
That melts me till depths leaving electrified...."

Passion paradise

Distracts me is your concealed figure,

Abstract I owe to conceit in vigour.

Drown me down in your heavenly charms,

Crown me on your chest and your arms.

Drain all my love till the seasons pass,

Stain my honor with this reason across.

Quench my thirst till the peaks,

Drench my lips in your mighty cheeks.

Lingering like an unloved guest,

All that I need is to rest on your chest.

"My kisses will stain your skin……
Until your love consumes me……."

Only goal is his soul

His voice hits my heart with hollow thud,

Aiming my nerves and the stimuli of echoes heard.

Had I ain't get any other guy in this vast world?

How I managed to survive growing this old?

He penetrated such deep in my only soul,

Seems like he's born with this only goal.

Moment I could save myself from his every stroke,

He made me stifle with the emotions evoke.

"Words are less to praise you extoll……
Together we can make a whole……."

Shadows of my past

His one kiss is enough for any sinner to find

heaven,

My desires that have blossomed him had driven.

Watching his gleeful moods in the rains,

He exudes the love that makes me fall for him

again.

He may be the one hope that cannot last,

After all the one dealt in shadows of my past.

The only reason is him for which I survive,

That makes me all these longing seasons be alive.

*"His hands in mine making him my
tomorrow!
Let this love last & all the beatitude on
him bestow!*

Sole Soul of my Life

Naïve that you look but you're indeed ain't,

Thrive that I for your gorgeous acquaint.

Adamant is your love with shatterproof tie,

Stimulant is your every move that makes me die.

Pacify this ordeal of love distress,

Apple pie is your YES to me, oh Mistress.

Let's create an epoch of our dwelling date,

Being my best half and a lovely soulmate.

"My dear Daisy,
You drive me crazy…….
You are the flow that enlighten me till I
doubt my sanity…."

Heart's flight

Night after night as the hyacinth blossom,

I saw his hair and his feet earthed bottom.

His lips were red,

As lilies dipped in red blood.

His face was bright,

Lighting up my hearts flight.

He took me onto his arms and danced the whole

dusk;

Kissed me deep,

Letting my soul drew out of sleep.

"Date unleft in dreams......
The hunt for you often screams......"

About the Author

Amaravathi is a writer who has started her work in recent times and she is a post graduate in English literature who love to engage herself in penning up poetries with a palpable spark, that are resultants of outflow of her emotions in order to create a romantic arena in readers hearts.

You can contact the Publisher at:
www.fanatixx.in